A Note to Parents

Read to your child...

★ Reading aloud is one of the best ways to develop your child's love of reading. Read together at least 20 minutes each day.

★ Laughter is contagious! Act out the story. Show your child that reading is fun.

★ Take time to answer questions your child may have about the story. Linger over pages that interest your child.

...and your child will read to you.

★ Follow cues from your child to know when he wants to join in the reading.

★ Support your young reader. Give him a word whenever he asks for it.

★ Praise your child as he progresses. Your encouraging words will build his confidence.

You can help your Level 1 reader.

★ Show your child how to handle a book. Show her the title and where the story begins.

★ Ask your child to find picture clues on each page. Talk about what is happening in the story.

★ Point to the words as you read so your child can make the connection between the print and the story.

★ Ask your child to point to words she knows.

★ Let your child supply the rhyming words.

W9-AHE-299

Library of Congress Cataloging-in-Publication Data

Goldowsky, Jill L.
    Dad's big idea / by Jill L. Goldowsky ; illustrated by Renée Andriani.
        p. cm. – (All-star readers. Level 1)
Summary: A boy and his friends like to make noise when they get
    together, but when his father is worried they will wake the baby, he helps
    them build a tree house to play in.
    ISBN 0-7944-0225-9
    [1. Tree houses—Fiction. 2. Fathers and sons—Fiction. 3. Stories in
rhyme.] I. Andriani, Renée, ill. II. Title. III. Series.

PZ8.3.G5698 Dad 2003
[E]—dc21   2002036861

Dad's Big Idea

by Jill L. Goldowsky
illustrated by Renée Andriani

All-Star Readers®

Reader's Digest Children's Books™
Pleasantville, New York • Montréal, Québec

I like to play with all my toys.

My friends come over. We make lots of noise!

We sing in the kitchen.

Bang drums in the den.

Shout, "Ready for take-off!"

on a countdown from ten.

Dad says, "Shhh!
There's too much noise.
The baby's sleeping.
Put away the toys."

Where can we go?
Where can we play?

"I have an idea!" I hear
Dad say.

He picks his toolbox
up from the floor.

He says, "Follow me kids,"

and walks out the door.

We all go outside.
What could this be?

We take a few steps.
We're under a tree!

Dad cuts us some wood.
We give him a hand.

We build together…

...a tree house—how grand!

We get a ladder.
We paint the sides.

Dad paints the top.

We go up inside!

We play with my toys.

It's like playing in space.

I love my tree house.

It's my own special place!

Color in the star next to each word you can read.

☆ a

☆ all

☆ and

☆ away

☆ baby

☆ bang

☆ be

☆ big

☆ build

☆ can

☆ come

☆ dad

☆ den

☆ door

☆ drums

☆ floor

☆ follow

☆ get

☆ hand

☆ he

☆ his

☆ I

☆ idea

☆ in

☆ inside

☆ make

☆ me

☆ much

☆ my

☆ noise

☆ of

☆ on

☆ out

☆ outside

☆ paint

☆ picks

☆ place

☆ play

☆ put

☆ ready

☆ says

☆ shout

☆ sing

☆ the

☆ too

☆ toys

☆ tree

☆ up

☆ walks

☆ we